ZOO SONG

by BARBARA BOTTNER

illustrated by LYNN MUNSINGER

SCHOLASTIC INC.
New York Toronto London Auckland Sydney

ISBN 0-590-33773-4

Text copyright © 1987 by Barbara Bottner.

Illustrations copyright © 1987 by Lynn Munsinger.

12 11 10 9 8 7 6 5 4 3 2   0 1 2 3 4/9

Printed in the U.S.A.   23

To my nice Jewish doctor

— B.B.

For Arlene

— L.M.

FABIO, HERMAN, and GERTRUDE were neighbors.

Gertrude had a terrible voice, but she loved to sing.

Whenever Gertrude began a song, Herman
would rattle the bars on his cage noisily. But she
never missed a note. The more he rattled, the
louder she sang.

"She's getting *louder*," Herman worried. She was.

"I must get her to stop making that awful noise."

Herman threw an orange at her. Gertrude
thought it was a present. But she did not want to
stop singing to eat the orange. So she merrily
threw it back.

One door over, Fabio, a quiet fellow, was minding his own business when he was hit by the flying orange.

"That lion!" he said.

He grabbed a pail and heaved it next door.

Zl-ammmm!!! It crashed and banged and rolled
on the floor. Herman roared in protest.

Gertrude thought, He is trying to drown me
out! She trilled in her highest soprano.

"I'll go crazy," moaned Herman. He banged against his door.

"I wish that lion would calm down," Fabio sulked.

Herman began to cry.

Gertrude continued to sing.

A man passed by and saw Herman crying. He played a cheery song on his violin. Then the man gently put the instrument in Herman's cage. "Here," he said. "You look like you need this more than I do."

Herman stopped crying and reached for the instrument.
He took the bow and stroked the violin.

It rasped, it warbled, it screeched.

Herman thought it was glorious.

He practiced his violin all afternoon and straight through dinner.

Gertrude thought she had never heard anything so awful. "But a true artist must never stop," she exclaimed. "No matter what!" So she sang all the louder to drown him out.

Fabio gloomily stared at the big, peaceful blue sky, wondering if the noise would ever stop.

A girl came by and saw Fabio's long face. She thought a dance might help him forget his troubles. Rat-ta-ta ta-ta-do da-doo went her nimble feet on the pavement.

But Fabio's face did not change.

The dancer bent down, untied her shoes, and gave them to Fabio. "You look like you need these more than I do," she said.

Fabio looked at the shoes. Why not? He stuffed his great bear paws into them.

As soon as they were on his feet, a new Fabio was born. He was filled with a rhythm he didn't know was in him. His quiet ways left him. He danced all night and never slept a wink.

Neither did Herman and Gertrude.

Gertrude shrilled on.

Herman sawed his bow over the violin strings with great purpose.

Fabio danced rat-tat-tat-tat-ta-too fast and furiously.

And all night long the zoo was noisy.
Very, very noisy.

But just as night turned into morning, something strange happened. Herman found a lovely melody on his violin. Gertrude sang the harmony—softly. Fabio danced the rhythm.

Herman, Gertrude, and Fabio hit the same notes,
the same beats, exactly.

When it was over, everyone stopped playing.
All was quiet. Very, very quiet.

Then Gertrude took a deep breath. She felt another song coming on. She sang the beginning, which was slow, and rather nice, Herman thought.

"Mind if I join in?" he asked.

"I'd be delighted," she said.

Herman picked up his violin.

"Fabio, will you give us the beat?" asked Herman.

"Don't mind if I do." Clicka clicka went Fabio's feet. "How I love to dance!"

Gertrude, Herman, and Fabio sang and danced the
very same song. They thought they sounded truly
wonderful. They didn't really. But then again, they
never knew, because they were all playing together.